THE RED BANDANA

A Western

R. Annan

One Vision Publishing
eBook ISBN: 978-1-942338-35-2
Print Book ISBN: 978-1-942338-34-5

Cover photo by L. Annan

Westerns by R. Annan:

Fight for the Lazy M
The Gunfighter in Winter
Long Ride to Hell's Kitchen
Owl Hawks
Gunfight at Barfield Springs
Shootout at Sanctuary City
Last Days of a Gunfighter

Coming Soon: Clay Jared Westerns

To

Fans of the Western Genre

1.

"Tommy, wait!"

Tommy Watt's sister Bessy stopped him as he was about to walk out the door.

"What is it, Sis?"

She had her hands behind her back, hiding something and smiling at him.

"I made this special for the dance," Bessy said as she brought out a bright red bandana she'd made by hand from a piece of cloth she bought in Storeyville.

Tommy Watt's eyes sparkled when he saw it. All the girls at the dance would surely notice him now, especially a certain blonde. The bandana was bright red with four white stars sewn one on each corner. He knew it would make him look rugged and daring.

When Bessy learned that her twin brother was going to the Harvest Moon dance over at Orlof's ranch she wanted to make him look special for the girls.

She told her mother her plans and they went all the way to Gabler's Mercantile in Storeyville to pick out the special piece of linen for the bandana. It was to be a big one, 27 by 27 inches and bright red with a white star sewn into each corner.

Tommy's father and mother watched as Bessy tied the bandana around her brother's neck. When she was done, she adjusted it so that a white star of the triangle was in front and pointing down, covering his prominent Adam's apple.

Tommy's mother stared at her pride and joy. An awkward, skinny kid of seventeen with pimples going to his first barn dance. Finally, she kissed him on the cheek.

He waved at his father.

"See ya later, Paw."

Smiling proudly at his mother and sister, he went out the door.

The young boy walked across the dark yard to the barn where his father had already saddled up the horse. A cold wind followed him in. Tommy shivered, mounted up and nudged the horse into a fast walk from the barn, across the yard, onto the road that led through Baker's Hollow towards Orlof's farm and finally on to Storeyville.

Although it was only five in the evening, winter's darkness had settled on the landscape. The moon was still hidden far below the horizon and yet to rise.

When he came to a place five miles on, the boy urged his horse into a rapid trot. He wanted to get through the deep depression called Baker's Hollow. Legend had it that all six members of the Baker family had been murdered there one night while coming back from town.

Although it was only a few hundred yards long, it had a downward slant that took the rider deep into a swampy landscape where vines and bushes grew dense in the summer and turned to a tangle of skeletons in the winter. Even then, the sun rarely penetrated into Baker's Hollow.

It was believed to be haunted by the angry spirits of the Baker family, and every time the boy ventured through, be it day or night, he thought he heard voices and saw shadowy shapes moving there.

It seemed to him to be miles long, as if it would never end, but the boy finally came out on the other side with a sigh of relief. He was now only three miles from the Orlof farm. Anxious to get there before the fun ended, the boy urged his horse into a fast gait.

Soon he sighted the Orlof farmhouse up ahead and the light coming from the windows of its huge barn. In a matter of minutes, he was in the yard tying his horse to a tree. The yard was full of buckboards and horses, and he had to zigzag his way to the barn door. He stepped in and looked around.

Gun belts were hung on pegs on either side of the entrance and chairs were lined up along the walls facing the dance floor. At the back end two fiddlers, a banjo player and a man on a mouth harp played a lively square dance.

Just inside the entrance to the right was a long table filled with food and drink. There were jugs of homemade cider as well as a large bowl of peach punch. Alongside this were trays of small sandwiches, cookies and fruits.

But the young boy's eyes were on the chairs where he soon saw the object of his desire, Miss Lilly Townsend, a sixteen-year-old, freckle-faced blonde beauty who would stand out in any crowd.

Tommy was mesmerized by her youthful beauty and for a moment could not move at all. Finally, the gangly, pigeon-toed boy spit on his hands, slicked back his dark brown hair and approached the chair of Miss Townsend.

"Kin I have this dance, Miss Lilly?" he asked, trying to sound casual. He adjusted his new, bright red bandana to call attention to it. It caught the young beauty's interest and she smiled.

"Sure, Tom," Miss Townsend said.

She went with him onto the dance floor, and for the rest of the night they danced every dance. His feet never touched the ground. He and Lilly Townsend danced and danced until the music ended.

Before she went to join her parents, Tommy Watts said, "Kin I call on ya sometime, Lilly?"

"Sure, Tom," Lilly said, and then ran over to leave with her family.

The young boy had never felt happier. He put his hand to his neck to feel the bandana, making sure it was there. It gave him confidence and brought him good luck, too. All his sister's love had gone into it and that made it special. He vowed never to take it off except when absolutely necessary.

One of the last to leave, the boy grabbed an apple from the table and went outside in the cold winter night. As he left, the lights went out in the barn and the doors closed.

He mounted up and pointed his horse towards home.

The wind was moaning across the yard and the moon was out of sight except for a small red tip just above the swaying pines. The night was getting blacker. Coyotes wailed somewhere back in the hills. By the time Tommy Watts came to Baker's Hollow it was pitch dark and he was suddenly very afraid.

He was halfway down the incline when it happened. It was very quick and it came out of nowhere.

Someone took hold of the horse's bridle and yanked its head sideways. The startled animal bucked. Tommy hung on until someone grabbed him, pulled him down and slammed a rock against the side of his head.

Many hours later, when he didn't come home, Tommy's father hitched up the buckboard and went looking for him. At dawn he found the boy's body down in Baker's Hollow. A bloody rock lay in a pool of blood next to Tommy's head. His attackers had taken every piece of his clothing, including the red bandana, and left a bedraggled prison uniform in its place.

That was the day the snowstorm hit the area. It would snow for days and cover up the tracks of the criminal or criminals who murdered young Tommy Watts.

Tommy's twin sister Bessy took his death especially hard, much more than anyone else did. It was believed it was because twins are more closely connected than other human beings.

2.

Two days before the barn dance there was a break at Storeyville Prison, twenty miles away. Six inmates managed to escape and once out they scattered in all directions. Two of them, Jocko Mintz and Speedy Jordan, headed south into farm country.

Mintz was a hulking giant of a man while Jordan was short and stocky. Both were cold-blooded murderers.

Ten miles from the prison they stopped to catch their breath. The thin material of their prison uniforms was no barrier against the winter wind. They were looking for a place to steal some heavier clothing.

"Where are we?" asked Mintz.

"We're near the Orlof farm. I know the area," Jordan said.

"Good. We'll steal us a horse an' head fer Texas. Maybe we kin make it over tha Mex border."

"Yeah," Jordan replied. "That'd be great."

They ran all that first night and were exhausted by dawn. They hid in the woods back behind the Orlof ranch and watched the activities going on.

"Looks like they're getting ready fer a party," Mintz said.

"Most likely a barn dance," Jordan replied.

Waiting in the woods while hoping for a chance to steal some food, they watched as people came in buckboards and on horses. They heard voices call out greetings to people. A marshal was there, as were other important people from the area. Cowboys with guns came by the dozens.

As the two convicts started for the farmhouse they were surprised by a dog. It sent them running again. After crossing several small streams, they passed through stands of aspen and birch and came to a road leading through a deep hollow not far from the Orlof farm.

"I gotta rest," Jordan said as he sank down on the hard frozen ground.

"Maybe we kin jump somebody comin' through here, Jordan," Mintz said. "Somebody is bound ta come through."

"Yeah. Get a horse and money," Jordan agreed.

They stepped off the road into the woods. Jordan picked up a rock and they squatted close together in the cold to keep warm, their teeth chattering. It was soon dark. Sometimes they dozed off as they waited. A hunter's moon passed across the sky above them and dropped out of sight below the far horizon. It was pitch dark in the hollow.

"Psst!" Mintz nudged Jordan awake. "Someone is coming!" he whispered.

Mintz, then Jordan, stood up and looked up to where the road slanted down. A figure on a horse was coming towards them. A coyote howled a long way off. The two convicts stood at the edge of the road and waited.

Big Jocko Mintz was the first to move. He leaped out, grabbed the horse's bridle, and held fast. The startled animal shrieked in alarm and bucked. Speedy Jordan pulled the rider from the saddle and swung the rock with all his might. There was a sickening sound and the rider fell dead at his feet.

"Get his clothes!" Mintz yelled as he tried to calm the horse down.

A few seconds later Jordan gasped.

"Christ! It's a kid! I jest killed a kid!"

It started to snow.

"Well, it's too late ta cry about it," Mintz growled. "Jest git his damn clothes!"

Jordon put on the boy's boots, pants, shirt, jacket and hat. When he saw the red bandana, it caught his eye. The little white stars seemed to dance. He quickly removed it from the boy's neck and tied it around his own.

They finally managed to get the horse calmed down and mounted up with the smaller Jordan sitting behind the cantle, his arms around the bigger man's waist to keep from falling off.

As they rode east toward Junction City, it began to snow harder. It slowed them down considerably. They hid out several times, once at a line shack where they found some scraps of food, and once in a barn outside a cluster of sod huts. They stole what food they could, when they could, and managed to get some clothes for Mintz off a clothesline.

They also argued a lot, and soon tempers began to flare.

"How come you always git ta ride in the saddle?" Jordan asked, sulking like a spoiled kid.

"Because I'm too big an' heavy ta ride rump!"

Jordan continued to be very unhappy with being jolted about on the ass end of a horse, but he said no more about it. What really bothered him was that they were moving too slowly. He was worried that a posse would catch up to them, and he would hang for murdering that young boy. Mintz would squeal on him like a stuck pig.

It also struck Jordan that without Mintz he could make the Mexican border much quicker alone.

One night, after a long, cold, grinding day, they found another empty line shack at the edge of a ranch. It had a good supply of food for the winter crew. Mintz and Jordan decided to hole up for the night and leave in the morning with as much food as they could carry.

It was there that Jordon found the skinning knife. While his friend Mintz was asleep, he stabbed him in the heart twice, packed up and rode off on his own.

He was still in Kansas when the posse caught up with him in a field near Brent's Ford. Before they hung him, Jordan confessed to murdering Tommy Watts. He also told them where to find Mintz's body.

Elroy Thomas, a young cowboy in the posse, took notice of the red bandana tied around Jordan's neck.

"Thet belonged ta the kid, didn't it, you son of a bitch?"

"Yes," Jordan answered.

"Give it over! It's goin' back."

Jordan untied the bandana and handed it to the cowboy who stuffed it in his denim jacket.

"Tell his family I'm right sorry fer what I did," Jordan whined. The cowboy nodded.

They found a tree near the edge of the field and hung Speedy Jordan as the snow fell, leaving him swaying in the wind. After that, they made camp in the aspens for the night. In the morning they cut the body down, tied it over a packhorse and went to get Mintz. Then they headed back to Storeyville.

It was getting colder and the wind sent the snow spiraling across the landscape. It howled in the pines and drove the snow down the necks of the posse. The men pulled their collars up and their hats down. They were glad to be heading home.

The cowboy, Elroy Thomas, suddenly found his denim jacket wasn't up to the job of keeping him warm. Its short collar let in the cold and the snow.

After a while, he could no longer bear the discomfort and took the red bandana from his pocket and tied it over the worn, faded one he had on. In a few moments he felt warmer.

No one took notice of what he had done, and after a while even Thomas forgot he had it on.

But one day, a stranger took notice of it. That would turn out to be the worst day in Elroy Thomas's life.

3.

After he was brutally murdered, Tommy Watt's twin sister had a nervous breakdown and never fully recovered. She wandered around in a daze for weeks and started talking in tongues. She would stare at the wall in her bedroom and babble incoherently for hours until she fell on the floor trembling and foaming at the mouth.

She couldn't go to school, so her father locked her in her room and only let her out to clean up and eat. She tried to kill herself, so they had to make sure there were no sharp objects where she could to get them.

Once she escaped from her room. They searched for her for two days and finally found her down in Baker's Hollow, half frozen to death. She was also bruised and cut up. When they brought her home, her father chained her to her bed.

She cried for hours and tore her clothes off and banged her head against the door in her room and moaned and wailed until she fell to the floor exhausted. When people talked to her she didn't seem to understand a word.

They brought in a doctor to cure her. He made her sit in a tub of ice cold water for hours until she turned blue. When that didn't help, they brought in a pastor to drive the evil spirits from her body and mind. He lashed her back with a cat-o-nine-tails until it was raw. Her mother couldn't stand it and sent the holy man away.

Finally, Bessy Watt's parents resigned themselves to the fact that their daughter was insane. They decided to have her put away.

"Bessy, my love," her mother said as she sobbed, "you have to go away. Do you understand, my sweet?"

Bessy Watts only looked at her mother with dull eyes and nodded.

The night before they were to take her to the institution for the insane, Bessy ran away. This time she made it as far the old Ellsworth to Sharon Springs coach road and collapsed. She laid on the seldom used road for two days before a small group of covered wagons and buckboards came by. They found her standing in her nightgown in the middle of the road, speaking in tongues. They were a small religious sect on their way to the mountains near Cheyenne Wells to start a new life.

The women of the sect took the girl under their care, cleaned her up and fed her. In a few days she settled down and became coherent. She told them about her brother's murder and how she had gone crazy. She remembered that her parents were going to send her to an institution for treatment and told them about the ice baths. She showed them the scars on her back put there by the good pastor.

"Stay with us, child," their leader, a kindly old man, said.

His name was Jacob, and Bessy Watts stayed with them.

4.

Elroy Thomas was living off his girlfriend Ella Neely who worked in the Silver Tip Saloon in the town of Storeyville outside the Storeyville Prison.

He was a cowboy by trade but had a lazy side when it came to work. Thomas could read and often read pulp magazines about men who were fast on the draw. These stories inspired him to practice his own quick draw skills at the edge of town. Ella, of course, paid for the ammunition. She bought her lover a new Colt for his thirtieth birthday.

"You should git a job, honey," Ella often told Thomas. "We could git married and settle down."

"Sure, baby, an' I will when the right job comes along," the cowboy always said to placate her.

When Thomas heard about the breakout at Storeyville Prison, he decided to join the posse to get away from Ella's constant carping. It paid five dollars a day. A cook and a packhorse with food would go along too.

There were extra horses to bring back the dead bodies, whoever they might be. Ella was also glad to get Thomas out of her hair for a while, so his going away suited them both. One snowy morning he kissed her and left.

When Thomas returned a week later with several double eagles in his Levis and looking handsome in his new red bandana, Ella rushed into his arms and kissed him.

"I was worried about you, honey. How did it go?" she asked.

"Nothin' much happened, baby," Thomas had wanted to show off his fast draw but never got the chance.

Ella's eyes fastened on the bright red bandana.

"Where did ya git thet pretty red bandana, honey?"

"I picked it up in Cheneyville, baby."

He had no intention of giving it to Tommy Watt's folks. It felt like a part of him now.

It was a week later that he heard about a man called Slade Colter, a famous bounty hunter and notorious fast draw. The Kansas City Star printed articles about Colter once a month.

"He must be makin' big money," Thomas told Ella.

"Ya think so?"

"Oh sure," Thomas said. "I bet thet newspaper pays him big money."

Ella shrugged. "Yeah, but what kind a life is it ta have gunnies comin' at ya every day? Thet can't be no fun."

"He stays at a hotel in Junction City," Thomas said. "He has this writer who follows him wherever he goes and writes it all down then sends it to Kansas City."

Ella suddenly looked frightened.

"Forgit about this Colter fellah, darlin'," she said. She kissed him and held him tight. "The kind a life he's a leadin' ain't fer us."

Elroy Thomas didn't answer. He smiled over her shoulder as she clung to him trembling with fear. The cowboy was thinking of fortune and fame that awaited him in Junction City.

A few days later Ella woke up to find a note on the nightstand next to the bed.

"I'm gonna make us rich, baby," it read.

She began to cry.

5.

Slade Colter was having his noon meal in the dining room of the Junction City Hotel when a young boy came in with a written message from someone named Elroy Thomas. He wanted Slade to meet him on the street at two in the afternoon.

Colter read the note and nodded.

"What did he look like, kid?"

"A cowboy," was all the boy said.

Colter handed the boy a quarter eagle.

"Tell him I'll be there as soon as I finish eating."

The boy ran off. Slade chuckled and turned to the small, bookish man with glasses across the table from him.

"Are you ready for another one, Mr. Turley," he asked.

"Yes sir, Mr. Colter," the young man said.

Mark Turley, a young aspiring writer for the Kansas City Star, was Slade Colter's camp follower and biographer. He gazed at Colter with an eager look.

The gunslinger was very tall, well over six feet and had a lanky, almost boney body. His coal black hair was combed flat on his overlarge head. Colter's eyes had a crazy look to them and blazed like hot coals under a large protruding forehead. The man's cheekbones stuck out on the sides of his face, almost showing through the skin. They framed his flat nose, wide mouth and jutting chin.

Slade Colter was just plain ugly and his face gave small children nightmares.

To offset this grotesqueness, Colter dressed in black from head to toes in fancy leather clothes. His black hat was adorned with small silver imitation conchas. His vest was decorated with silver buttons and tiny chamois straps, matching his coal black leather boots.

He wore two Colts in an ornate gun belt with twin holsters. The one on the left was mostly for show. It was the right one that he dealt death with and it got the job done quickly.

Mark Turley was writing in his ledger that Colter just got his twenty-second challenge from an unknown aspiring cowboy wanting to steal Colter's title as the fastest draw in the territory. Whenever a challenge took place, Turley would stand on the sidelines. He watched every move Colter made and wrote a glowing description of how his idol destroyed the challenger. He would heap praise and glory on the man.

After all, Slade Colter was his bread and butter.

Colter finished his meal off with a shot of brandy. He stood up and took his black leather gloves off the table and put them on. After yawning and stretching, almost as if he was sleepy and bored, the gunslinger checked the cylinder of the Colt on the right side. He smiled at Turley.

"Let's go, Mr. Turley."

Colter walked with sure, measured steps out onto the porch of the Junction City Hotel and looked up at the winter sky. It was blue, the sun was bright and most of yesterday's snow had melted from the road leaving the street puddled and muddy.

A cowboy stepped off the plank sidewalk down by the barbershop about fifty feet away. He stood in the middle of the road and waited. Colter nodded to him as he stepped down from the porch.

People on the street scattered. It emptied in seconds.

Colter walked a few feet closer to a spot in the road where he felt comfortable. This was his killing spot, where he would make it all happen, forty feet from his prey.

"What's yer name, cowboy?"

"Thomas. Elroy Thomas."

"Where ya from, Thomas?"

"Near Storeyville."

"No, I mean, where were you born?"

"Simpson's Gulch, over by the Pawnee River."

Turley wrote furiously in the ledger that Colter was being braced by the notorious Pawnee Kid. This was how they worked it. It had to be high drama. Colter would get the name and birthplace of the challenger, quickly kill him and Mark Turley would embellish the whole story. It had to be sensational or it wouldn't sell.

"Ready. Mr. Thomas?" Colter yelled down the road to the cowboy.

Elroy Thomas nodded. Suddenly his mouth was too dry to speak. His heart pounded against his ribs. Here he was, on the street of Junction City, facing the famous Slade Colter, the king of the fast draw. If he could pull it off he would be the man, the one they would write stories about in all the big city newspapers. Colter would soon be only a footnote in the past. Thomas would ride the wave.

The cowboy drew without warning, thinking he would catch the gunslinger off balance but it didn't work out quite as he planned. His gun was out but didn't make it up to gut level.

A bullet beat the roaring blast of Colter's Colt and slammed into the cowboy's heart.

Thomas looked up at the sky for a moment and thought he saw Ella's smiling face. Everything went white for a second and then quickly drifted into black. People on the sidewalks saw the cowboy's knees buckle and watched in awe as he fell like a sapling cut down with one blow of an axe.

What had taken but a few seconds to happen was quickly entered in Mr. Turley's ledger in flowing words of romantic grandeur. An epic event just took place and must be recorded for posterity, for the many fans who followed the adventures of western gunfighter Slade Colter.

Colter holstered his Colt and strutted slowly down the road. Several men and women quickly gathered around the cowboy's body. When they saw Colter coming they shrunk away in fear. He seemed to be the black specter of death coming their way.

Colter stared down at the body of Elroy Thomas, also known as the Pawnee Kid. He tilted his head and nodded. Suddenly he noticed the red bandana and was instantly attracted to it. For some reason it seemed to reach out to him and he couldn't turn away.

"Get the bandana, Mr. Turley," Colter said. "Have it washed and ironed and then bring it to me.

"Of course, Mr. Colter," Turley said.

He shoved his ledger under his left arm and bent down and untied the bandana from the dead man's neck.

A bank of clouds suddenly blocked out the sun and a cold wind blew up the street. Turley shivered, got up and ran after Slade Colter who was walking swiftly towards the hotel.

6.

The rider was caught out in the open.

Thick flakes of snow fell in a shimmering blanket all about him, coming down so fast he couldn't see more than fifty feet ahead. The horse didn't like it either but kept going straight on. There was no other way to go, nothing else to do.

Sometimes a blast of winter wind blindsided the rider and his horse, almost bowling them over. The young cowboy gripped the saddle horn and leaned against the buffeting blast to keep from being slapped off into the deep snow.

The wind howled like a wounded banshee.

A few yards on and the horse stepped into a gopher hole and went down with a shriek of pain. When the rider heard the bone snap in the animal's front right leg, he knew it was all over. As the horse went over on its right side the rider tried to slide out and away to avoid being pinned under. He was too slow and didn't make it.

He went down with the horse as it slid sideways into a shallow gully and came to a stop.

For a moment he lay there not believing his bad luck. Then he realized his right leg was wedged under the horse's right flank, tight as a drum.

Somewhere, not far away, a wolf howled.

"Get up, boy!" the cowboy yelled in pain. His leg was going numb.

The horse tried to rise up to help him but screamed and fell back every time, crushing the rider's leg even more. The cowboy moaned and sucked in air to stop from passing out. The horse finally gave up and lay gasping in pain.

The young cowboy turned his hips so he could get at his Colt. He got it out and shot the horse in the back of its head, cursing himself and sobbing. After the last echo of the gunshot had died away, a wolf howled again, closer this time. Another wolf answered with a long wail.

The cowboy struggled to get his Winchester out of the sheath under the horse. He grabbed the stock and pulled, struggling against the dead weight of the animal. Finally, it slid up and out. The cowboy jammed the barrel under the animal's flank and pushed upward on the stock. After several futile attempts he was able to leverage the flank high enough to slide his leg out.

He stood up, rubbing and slapping his leg to get the blood circulating again, stomping his boot heel against the hard frozen ground. Finding nothing was broken he quickly removed the saddle and other gear from the horse, all the while choking back tears.

"I'm sorry, old friend," he kept repeating. "Forgive me old pal."

Finally, when he had all his gear including his lariat, he started off towards a distant stand of pine trees, dragging his saddle and gear in the snow. Halfway to the trees he heard more howling. He stopped to look back.

Three wolves were loping towards him through the deep snow. For a moment the young cowboy stared in awe, then dropped the saddle and sat down on it.

He sat there as if hypnotized, watching the smooth fluid movement of the beasts coming to tear him apart. He had heard they went for the throat first. Little white puffs of steam came from their snouts as they labored along, eager to get at him. The muscles rippled in their shoulders and flanks as they fought to overcome the deepness of the snow. The leader was a big fellow with red eyes that blazed against the whiteness of the falling flakes.

Suddenly they veered to the right and headed to where the horse lay.

"You can't have him, you sons a bitches!" the cowboy screamed.

He sighted along the barrel of his Winchester and fired off three rounds.

7.

The snowstorm had all but blotted out any sign of the Junction City to Ellsworth road. This slowed down the strange looking coach that was making its way west. On its doors were the initials F.R. in gold capital letters.

Up on top were two cowboys. One drove the two-horse team while the other rode shotgun with a Winchester. The cab inside was richly appointed with plush tanned leather seats. The doors had glass windows to keep out the noise and the elements.

The lone passenger inside was a woman of extraordinary beauty. Her abundant auburn hair was in a bun tucked under her wide brimmed bonnet. She had large blue eyes set above a perfectly beautiful red mouth. Her nose was perfect, as well. The coat she wore was mink fur and her dress was black velvet. On her feet were high-heeled shoes. She was no woman of the west. Everything about her spoke of a high city life, mansions and balls. Yet there was something about her that exuded strength and world experience.

As the coach made its way slowly through the falling snow, she often fixed her eyes on the world outside. At times she heard the howl of a wolf and looked for it but there was nothing to see but the dull, boring, whiteness outside. It had been like that for miles now.

Then, up ahead where the road curved to the left, she saw a lone cowboy walking by the side of the road carrying his saddle and gear. His head was bent low as he headed into the wind. His hat and the shoulders of his denim jacket were covered with snow.

As the coach went by, he turned to stare in at her. For a long moment she saw his young, handsome face. Their eyes met. He smiled and then was gone from sight but the image of him stayed with her. He was, she thought, perhaps two, three, maybe four years younger than her thirty years.

She was still thinking of him about half a mile down the road when she saw two riders off to the side in a nearby stand of pine trees with their rifles pointed in her direction. A few seconds later she heard two moans from above, followed by the echoing roar of two rifle shots. The coach driver and his companion toppled down into the snow.

The sudden blasts from the rifles spooked the horses. They bolted and sped off into the blinding snow. Fifty feet on they ran off the road into a ditch. The coach flipped over on its right side. The frightened horses dragged it a few yards, until it hung up on something and then stopped.

Both riders spurred their mounts up to the coach. One dismounted and opened the left side door. Just as he looked in the woman shot him between the eyes with a derringer she had hidden in her purse.

The other cowboy pulled his gun and fired a random shot into the coach. He was about to fire a second shot when a bullet from fifty feet away hit him between the shoulder blades. He spun forward out of his saddle onto the ground near his companion.

The young cowboy walked up to the coach. When he got close, a feminine voice yelled out to him.

"Leave me alone. I'm not going back!"

"They're all dead, ma'am," the cowboy said.

"Are you the cowboy we just passed?"

"Yes, ma'am."

"You killed the other one, didn't you?"

33

"Yep. Are you alright, ma'am?"

"I think so but I am a little bruised, sir."

"Can you git out?"

"Yes, if you would kindly help me."

The young cowboy looked into the coach and stared in at the woman as she put her derringer back in her purse and slung the strap over her shoulder. She smiled up at him. He grabbed her under her arms and lifted her up as if she were light as a feather.

He set her gently on the ground.

"Oh, dear, you're strong," she said, leaning against him and holding onto his arms while she caught her breath. Her face was close to his.

They stared into each other's eyes. The wind blew the fur collar of her coat against her flushed cheeks. He noticed how red her lips were against the backdrop of the white world around them.

"What's your name, cowboy?" she asked.

"Ed. Ed Barnes."

The woman laughed. It was such a common name for a cowboy. It seemed they were all named Ed or Rob or Jack.

"Well Edward," she said, "thank you for saving my life."

"My pleasure ma'am."

She looked around at the bodies.

"Are they all dead?"

"Yes, ma'am, they sure are."

"What shall we do then?"

"Well, we can't do very much ma'am," the cowboy said. "Can you ride?"

"Yes. I have ridden before."

"Then we'll go down the road ta find a town."

Before she could answer, the cowboy started to drag the snow covered bodies off to the side of the road. He unhitched the coach horses and tied their halters to the saddle straps of the mounts of the dead attackers.

When the lady saw this she said, "Won't that slow us down?"

"A little but we might need them ma'am. I jest lost my horse to a gopher hole a ways back."

"I see."

The cowboy cinched his own saddle and gear on one of the attacker's horses but kept the extra blankets, giving him a total of three.

Suddenly he had a thought and looked into the boot behind the coach. There he found two large bags of oats. He carried them over to one of the extra horses then cut a length from his rope lariat. He tied one end to each pack and slung it over one the back of one of the extra horses.

"Well ma'am, I guess thet's about all we kin do," he said.

He looked around as if he had forgotten something.

"Alright then let's go." She sounded urgent.

"Whose coach is thet ma'am?"

"My husband's."

"He'll be mighty anxious about you, won't he?"

She laughed sarcastically. "No. Actually, he's trying to kill me."

8.

It was harder to follow the road now because the snow was deeper. At times they wandered off into a gully and had to struggle to get all the horses back to level ground. The cowboy noticed the woman handled her mount well and had no problem keeping it under control.

An hour before nightfall they came up to a rise and stopped to look down at a town about a mile away. There was a wooden sign nailed to a scrub oak by the side of the road. The cowboy brushed the snow from it.

"What does it say?" he asked the woman. She realized he couldn't read.

"Danville. One mile."

"I'll take you there," the cowboy said. "They'll have a telegraph station. You kin send fer yer husband."

"No, I can't do that."

"Why not, ma'am?"

"I told you. He's out to kill me!"

The young cowboy didn't believe her. Perhaps she hit her head when the coach tipped over and wasn't in her right mind. He heard about things like that. When people got hit in the head they sometimes got funny. Some even forgot their names. But even so, he had no power to make her go there. And he certainly couldn't abandon her.

They rode down the hill. A hundred yards from the town, they turned left and went around it. They found the ruins of an old abandoned barn to the north.

Dismounting, they led the horses inside. Though it sagged, most of the roof was still in place and one far corner was protected by what was left of the walls. It was dry there and protected from the wind and snow.

"We'd best stay here for the night," the cowboy said. She looked around and nodded.

He tied the horses to an upright inside and put a pile of oats down for them to eat. Then he gathered up some broken barn boards and built a small fire. He got a little two cup coffee pot from his saddlebag and filled it with snow. When it began to steam he dropped in some coffee. He only had one bent tin cup so he let her drink the hot brew first. She laughed then took a sip and handed it back.

"This is fancy dining," she said, smiling. They ate some jerky and hardtack. "I read about this."

After they ate he gathered up all the scattered straw he could find and laid a blanket over it.

"You first, ma'am," he said.

She removed her bonnet, pulled the collar of her fur coat up about her ears and laid down. He lay next to her and pulled the other two blankets over them. They watched the fire as it burned down to glowing embers.

"I know you think I'm crazy but I'm not," she said.

"Ta be honest, I don't know how ta figure you out, ma'am. What's all this talk about someone tryin' ta kill you?"

"It's true. It's my husband. His name is Trey Ferguson and he's trying to murder me."

"What fer?"

"He wants me to sign over my half of our ranch to him. It was my father's ranch before I got married to Trey. Now he wants it all."

"What's it worth?"

"The ranch? Quite a lot. Eighty thousand, I suppose."

"Gosh!"

He went quiet for a moment mulling over what she said.

'My feet are freezing," she said and shivered.

"Ma'am, thet dress and shoes yer a wearin' are mighty pretty but they're useless out here. We gotta git you some real rags. Maybe I kin steal some off a clothesline in town."

"You don't have to steal anything, Edward," she said. I have plenty of money in my purse."

"Alright, then, I'll do it tomorrow."

She shivered again.

"Could I come closer?"

"Shucks yes, ma'am. Git as close as ya want."

She moved up close and put her head on his shoulder. He could smell her perfume and hair. For a moment he thought he might be dreaming. This couldn't be happening to him, a cowboy with no roots, a drifter from job to job. Soon she was asleep but he stayed awake until just before dawn when he nodded off. Later a rooster's call woke him up.

He made a fire and coffee again. She gave him a fifty-dollar bank note and he walked into town. An hour later he returned with a set of young boy's clothing, including boots and a wide brimmed hat. She was small but they fit her well enough. The fur coat went well with the wool shirt and pants. She almost looked like a trapper.

Now that she looked like a man, they rode into town for a real breakfast of bacon, eggs, grits, coffee and doughnuts. Before leaving, they went to the town mercantile and bought a bunch of stuff, including a slab of salted ham, salt, pepper, flour and sugar. Also a frying pan, two tin plates, two tin cups and some kitchen utensils. They put it in two sacks and tied them over the back of the second coach horse.

Now they had two saddled horses, two packhorses and looked like prospectors on their way to pan for gold.

That purse of hers sure had a lot of money in it.

9.

Trey Ferguson sat alone in the same kind of special made coach that his wife ran away in. On top sat a driver and a shotgun dressed in navy blue chauffeur uniforms. Large gold letters, F.R., which meant Ferguson's Ranch, were stenciled on the doors. And like his wife, he stared out at the passing white fields of solemn black trees hanging their branches in surrender to winter winds that buffeted them to and fro.

The snow slacked off a little and the sun was out which made the going easier on the old, now seldom used, Ellsworth to Junction City coach road.

As the coach came around a bend in the road Ferguson and his crew saw the companion coach overturned in the snow up ahead. They came alongside and stopped. The shotgun man jumped down and walked to it and looked inside.

"Is she in it Taggert?" Ferguson yelled.

"No boss! It's empty."

Taggert walked over to Ferguson.

"Somebody stole the two horses," he said.

"Where's the next town?" Ferguson asked.

"Danville. Just down the road."

"We'll go there and get something to eat and ask around," the rancher said. Taggert got up next to Bowles, the driver and they drove on.

"What about the bodies' boss?" Taggert yelled.

"Leave them for the wolves," Ferguson yelled back.

In half an hour they were in Danville talking to the owner of the beanery where the cowboy and his wife had eaten.

"Yeah, they was here," he said. "She was dressed like a boy but you could tell she was a woman. Pretty as a picture, she was."

They went down to the stable and talked to the man in charge about towing the coach in. Later, back in his private coach, the rancher swore. His face was purple with rage.

"That cheating bitch! I'll put an end to her this time!"

"The man at the beanery said the cowboy was wearing a gun, boss. We'd best be careful. She might have hired a gunslinger to protect her," Taggert said.

Ferguson thought about that for a moment. He looked at his private guard. "What do you suggest, Taggert?"

"I know a man who will take care of your problem, Mr. Ferguson. For a fee he'll take care of her too, I think. That is, if you want him to."

"Who is he?"

"Ever hear of Slade Colter?"

"No, not really."

"He was a bounty hunter once but now he's famous as a gunslinger. They write stories about him in the newspapers. He's the fastest in the territory."

"Can you get him out here to Danville?"

"I'll send a telegram to the hotel in Junction City where he hangs out most of the time."

"Do it now, then," Ferguson said anxiously. "Do it now and make it worth his while!"

10.

This strange woman puzzled the young cowboy. One moment she was thoughtful and meditative and the next moment she was smiling and outgoing. At other times she alternated between being serious and mature to foolish and childish. He never knew what to expect.

As they traveled west, she became more maternal towards him. One day when she saw a rip in his shirt, she had him remove it and give it to her so she could mend it with a small sewing kit she kept in her purse.

When she finished she stared at his naked torso. Her eyes sparkled in the light of the campfire. She put the palm of one hand on his chest where his heart was. Her soft touch made it beat faster. She smiled, knowing she had caused this.

"You are an Adonis," she said. "Perfect."

Blood rushed to his face and he blushed. When she saw that, she pulled her hand away and laughed. He quickly put on his shirt and jacket.

It snowed constantly all that day. Toward evening he found a dry hollow place under a huge pine tree. A place where they were able to crawl into. It was like a quiet little chamber. The cowboy tied the four horses in a sheltered area and went to work collecting feathery young branches to make a bed for the woman and himself.

After spreading one blanket over the branches and making a fire from dried pine needles, the cowboy filled the small coffee pot with snow and got it boiling. Moments later they had coffee, jerky and hard tack.

As he worked her eyes followed his every move as if she were watching something strange and new. He felt it and once he turned to look at her, their eyes connected in a mutual stare. It made him feel all warm inside. Again, she saw the effects and broke the spell with a laugh.

"Sit here," she said after they ate. She patted the blanket closer to her. "I want you to tell me all about yourself. Who you are. Where you come from."

The cowboy chuckled. Never in all his life had anyone been that interested in him.

"I'm jest a dumb cowboy, ma'am," he said. "I was raised on a sheep farm and ran away when I was fifteen ta be a cowboy. Thet's about all there is ta me. Heck, there ain't nothing interstin' about me at all."

"Have you killed men?"

"Yes, ma'am. I kilt my first one when I was seventeen."

"And after that?"

"Three."

"How old are you?"

"I ain't sure. Twenty-somethin', I guess."

She stared at his face. He looked about twenty-five.

"I'm thirty," she said. "My name is Helen."

"Helen?"

"Yes. Helen Ferguson." She stared at the flickering fire for a moment. "Can I tell you my story?"

"Yes, ma'am. Please do."

"My father was president of a large bank in Chicago," she said, staring into the flames. "It was a big cattlemen's investment bank. Wealthy cattlemen sent their money there to be invested in the stock market."

She looked to see if he was interest. He seemed to be.

"When I was sixteen, after my mother died, my father sent me to one of those fancy girl's finishing schools."

"In the city?"

"No. It was in upstate New York. After graduation I taught at a school in the city."

"An' yer dad?"

"He got what was known as cattle fever and decided to become a cattle baron. He sold the house in Chicago and went west to a small town in south Kansas, by the Oklahoma border. He bought a large ranch next to another very large ranch owned by a man named Trey Ferguson."

She paused again to make sure he was listening.

"Somewhere along the way my father and Trey formed a partnership. Together they called it the Fergusson O'Brien Ranch Combine. It was over a hundred square miles. I was teaching in New York at the time."

"Gosh!"

"Yes. Gosh, indeed."

"Yer paw was one of them cattle barons, then?"

"Yes, his dream finally came true at last."

"What happened then?"

"Well, he died a year later. I received a packet from the Cattlemen's Investment Bank in Chicago, where he was once president. In it was my father's last Will and Testament, naming me sole owner of his share of the ranch."

"Gosh! What did ya do then?"

"Nothing at first but then I got a letter from my father's partner, Trey, asking me to come west to see the ranch. He said he would have a private coach pick me up when I got off the train at Newton, Kansas."

"An' did he?"

"Yes and after a very long trip, I was finally at the ranch."

"I bet ya were happy about thet."

"At first I was. Trey swept me off my feet and wined and dined me. He said he wanted to make me the happiest woman in the world. Six months later we were married."

"An' now he wants to kill ya? Why?"

She stared back into the dying embers again and sighed.

"He wants me to sign my half of the ranch over to him. As long as I have my father's will, it will always be mine. At least forty percent, which is what my father owned, since his ranch was the smaller of the two."

She paused for a moment.

"Trey tried every trick in the book to get me to sign the deed over to him. He drugged me once and even threatened to have me declared insane. Finally, he said he would kill me. That's when I left."

"An' thet's when I came up on ya."

"Yes, thank God. I owe you my life."

That's when she first started the habit of kissing him. She pressed her lips softy on his and pulled back. Stroking his cheek with her fingers, she stared into his eyes and watched him blush. This became a habit with her.

That night as they lay huddled together under the blanket, after the fire had gone out, he thought about the story she told him. He didn't know whether to believe it or not. Why didn't she turn to the law for help? Or run back to New York? Or hire a lawyer in Chicago or Kansas? That would be the simplest thing to do.

But then, what did he know? He was just a stupid uneducated cowboy. Maybe she got scared and panicked. Maybe she was terrified for her life.

One thing was real and for certain, someone had tried to kill her. He was witness to that.

11.

"Edward," she said, looking serious.

"Yes, ma'am?"

"I'm going to take a bath."

They had happened upon an old abandoned miner's camp. About a hundred feet from the rundown deserted cabin was a small hot spring that sent up clouds of steam.

"Yes, ma'am."

"You must stand guard like a soldier to make sure no one comes," she said.

The cowboy chuckled.

"There's no one around here for miles, ma'am."

"Still, I'll take no chances, Edward. I want you here with me while I take a bath. Will you do that?"

"Yes, ma'am."

She removed her fur coat and spread it near the dry edge of the spring then began to undress. He looked away. She saw that and laughed.

"You don't have to be shy around me, Edward," she said. "You can look at me if you want. I'm not ashamed of the body God gave me. Neither should you be."

Still, he refused to look.

"Edward!" she demanded. "Look at me!"

He slowly turned to look at her.

"Am I not beautiful?"

His heart was pounding hard against his ribs. He was speechless and could only nod his head. His face was as purple as a beet.

She tested the water with one toe then stepped in until the water was up to her waist. Once there she sat down slowly and began running her hands over her body.

"Oh, this is wonderful, Edward," she said. "I wish I had soap. Soap would be nice."

He watched her clean herself until she finally stopped and looked in his direction.

"Go get me a blanket, please," she said.

He untied a blanket from a horse and stood with it at the edge of the spring but she didn't reach for it.

"Hold it up for me, please?" she asked.

He held the blanket out and open. He wrapped it around her as she came between his arms. She looked up into his eyes and kissed him lightly on the lips then stepped from his embrace, holding the blanket by herself.

When she had dried herself, she tossed the blanket to him and began dressing. His mind was reeling. He had never seen a woman like her. She was both beautiful and intelligent. If she was crazy, then he wished all women were as insane as she was.

They left the horses hobbled near some birch trees where winter grass poked through the snow and went into the ruins of the old prospector's cabin. Surprisingly the cedar board roof had held throughout the years and it was dry inside. He arranged the blanket over a wooden chair to dry.

There were two crudely made bunks with leather straps for springs. Helen sat cautiously on one. It held.

"This is nice," she said.

The cowboy looked around. A fireplace with a hearth made from fieldstone stood against one wall. It had a grate to cook on and an angle iron to hold a pot or kettle.

They got their saddlebags, rifles and supplies from the horses and brought them all in. Helen dusted off the chairs and small table while the cowboy made a fire in the hearth. The heat of it soon pushed the cold away.

"I'm goin' hunting," Edward said.

"Hunting? For what?"

"There's rabbit tracks all over the place."

"Oh, dear, poor little rabbits," she said.

He grabbed his Winchester and went out the door chuckling.

While he was gone Helen filled the coffee pot with snow and hung it from the angle iron, over the fire. She got out two salt and pepper boxes and put them on the table. Next, she put the frying pan on the grate and dropped a piece of fatty bacon in it to melt.

She poured a small amount of water from the coffee pot into a tin plate and mixed in some flour and salt until she had a firm batter. Forming them into several small patties, she dropped them into the frying pan. In half an hour she had a half dozen pan-fried biscuits. After that she dropped the coffee grounds into the coffee pot.

The cowboy returned in an hour with a large skinned rabbit that he had cut up into portions. She took it and rubbed the parts down with salt and pepper and placed it in the frying pan that was seasoned with bacon fat.

"My mouth is a waterin'." The cowboy said.

Finally, they sat down and ate their first hot meal in days. Helen opened a can of peaches for desert.

She smiled and said, "This is like a honeymoon."

He didn't know how to respond to that so he just chuckled and smiled back.

12.

A few days after arriving at the old abandoned cabin, they discovered another miner's operation going on about a half a mile below on the downward slope of the mountain. There were about twenty men, women and children there, all panning for gold by a rapidly flowing stream.

One sunny afternoon, Edward and Helen walked down to say hello. They were met by an old man with a shaggy head of hair and a long beard. His skin was weathered by exposure to the cold, wind and sun.

"When he saw them he was surprised. He put his pan down and walked over to greet them. The other people stopped work to stare.

"Howdy, strangers!" the old man cried out as if they were long lost relatives dropping in for a surprise visit.

Three children ran over to stand a few feet away and stare. A pretty young girl, about seventeen, stood at a sluice box staring at them, but mostly at the cowboy. Another girl came up to Helen and felt her fur coat as if it was something wonderful and mystic. The girl's mother rushed over. She grabbed the girl and pulled her away.

"We're up at the old cabin," Edward said, pointing up the slope. "We sorta got lost in the snowstorm a few days back."

"Where were ya headed, friends?" the old man asked.

"We're on our honeymoon," Helen said before the cowboy could answer.

The old man chuckled, but there was something in it that said he had his doubts.

"My wife's name is Helen," Edward said. "Mine is Ed."

"And I'm Jacob," the old man replied. "We're gonna be eatin' soon. Come sit with us. Do you like mutton stew with turnips?"

"We sure do," the cowboy said. Helen smiled and nodded in agreement.

The cowboy noticed the sheep pen over by a big barn-like building. Nearby he saw another long narrow building with a cross above the door. Next to it were what looked like several small bunkhouses Dozens of hens and roosters ran wild in the open area. Two cows stood in a small pen away from the sheep.

A dog came up and sniffed them.

They ate in the long narrow building with the cross over the door. Jacob explained that it was both their communal dining hall and church. The kitchen was in the room in the back.

Helen and Edward were given chairs at the head of the long table facing Jacob at the other end. After everyone had bowed their heads to say grace, three young girls came from the kitchen and filled everyone's tin cup with a mild apple cider.

"A toast," Jacob said, raising his cup. "To this newlywed couple. May the Lord bless their union with many children."

Everyone said Amen, pointed their cups towards Helen and Edward and drank.

After that the food was brought in. It was a simple meal with bowls of steaming mutton and turnip stew with butter and biscuits. It was delicious. For desert they had wild strawberry tarts topped with sour cream.

It was nearly dark when the meal was over. All the men went back outside while the women cleaned up.

Edward and Helen followed old Jacob outside to where several men were piling logs on a bonfire. Someone began to play a flute. The tone was soft and sweet. They sat at a bench by the fire talking.

"Is there a road nearby?" the cowboy asked.

"Yep," the old man replied. "There's an ol' coach road. It runs towards Ellsworth in the east and ta Oakley in the west. If ya goes fur enough west, it'll take ya into Cheyenne Wells in Colerady."

"How about a town?"

"Yep. Russellville. About five miles east. It ain't much. It use ta be a stage stop. Now it's mostly a hangout fer bad characters. I wouldn't go there, if I were you."

The cowboy nodded.

"I see you have a church," Helen said. "Do you have a pastor?"

Jacob chuckled.

"No, ma'am. I get ta do all the preachin'," he said. "An' the hitchin', too. I git ta do jest about everything when it comes ta the Lord an' the law, I guess."

"That must keep you very busy, Jacob," Helen said.

"Oh, it does, alright. It surely does."

They made idle talk for a while. The cowboy finally stood up. Helen and the old man did too.

She said, "Thank you for your hospitality, sir."

"My pleasure, ma'am," Jacob said. "Come anytime ya git the itch ta wonder." Helen smiled.

The cowboy and the woman walked slowly back up the slope towards the cabin. Once there they rebuilt the fire in the hearth and pulled the chairs close.

The cowboy chuckled. "The women kept starin' at yer fur coat."

"Yes, I did notice," Helen said. She laughed a little too. "What nice simple people. Out here, all alone."

"They seem happy, though."

"Yes, they do indeed," she said dreamily, staring into the fire. She moved her chair closer to his and put her head on his shoulder. "One of the young girls kept staring at you. She couldn't take her eyes off you, Edward."

"I never noticed."

"Liar. I'm jealous. I thought I was your only girl."

He didn't know how to answer that.

"Am I your only one, Edward? Your only girl?"

He turned to look at her.

"Please don't make fun of me, ma'am," he said. "I know I'm jest a dumb cowboy an' yer a lady."

She put a hand softly against his cheek.

"You're my cowboy, Edward and I'm your lady. I'll always be your lady if you want me. Do you want me?"

"You have ta stop talkin' like thet, ma'am. I know it's jest talk. It can't go nowhere."

"Yes it can, Edward," she said, looking into his eyes. "It can go wherever you take it."

She pulled his head down to her face and kissed him. This time it was a meaningful kiss that lasted a long time.

When it was done she said, "No one is ever going to take you away from me, Edward. No one, never."

13.

Helen Ferguson once was Helen O'Brien, born to a poor Irish family in the poor suburbs of Chicago. One of seven siblings, she had three brothers and three sisters. Of the girls, she was the oldest.

After school, Helen worked in a boarding house making beds and washing laundry. At night, she read romantic pulp magazine stories about poor girls who married rich men and princes. It seemed a wonderful thing to do but she knew it was just a fantasy.

No girl in her neighborhood had ever married above a teamster or skinner at a stockyard. One, though, did marry a bareknuckle boxer but then there were plenty of Irish boxers in almost every bar on the south side.

At an early age Helen became aware that boys stared at her constantly. By seventeen she realized why. The answer was in her mirror which revealed she was very pretty, if not beautiful. She also had the ability to read men's minds through the looks on their faces.

At the boarding house where she worked, if the man was young or handsome, she would give up a kiss for a coin. She put this extra money away in a secret place so her mother wouldn't take it from her. Over time she gathered a considerable cache of coins, from quarter eagles up to double eagles, which demanded more than just a kiss.

Young Helen had a dream of getting out of a house where the father was a notorious neighborhood drunk who usually stopped at a bar on his way home on paydays and spend most of the week's wages on gambling and drinks.

One day, one of Helen's girlfriends from school told her about a gambling casino uptown where girls were paid just to walk around looking pretty. Their job was to entice the customers to gamble and drink. The pay was good but you had to dress nice and wear perfume.

Helen obsessed about the casino for a month then decided to take her kissing money, buy a dress and go up there to apply for a job. And she did. She was eighteen but could look twenty when she wanted to. You could never tell with a girl anyway, what their age really was.

The man in charge took one look at Helen O'Brien and knew he had a moneymaker. He hired her on the spot.

It wasn't long before her mother found out and raised the roof. No daughter of hers would lead the life of sin while living in her house. Helen was now a little tart who was a disgrace to the O'Brien clan. She must either give up the casino job or move out.

Helen moved in with Susan, one of the girls working at the Blue Heron Casino. They became very close friends, almost like sisters and looked out for each other through good times and bad. After two years at the Blue Heron they heard about the cattle boom out west and traveled to St. Louis for a better job.

They did well there but Susan wanted to meet a better class of clientele. She was ready to get married and settle down. A rich rancher would be just fine. After a year in St. Louis, Helen and Susan took a train to Kansas City. It was there they met all the ranchers they could handle and more. In six months, Susan became the mistress of a rich one who set her up in her own apartment, paid all her bills and gave her a generous allowance besides.

When that happened, Helen was left on her own.

One day she met Gerald Oswald, a Kansas City lawyer. He was not a handsome man but he had manners and treated

Helen like a lady. He also paid the rent for her apartment above the casino and bought her expensive gifts. Like Susan's rancher, Oswald also was married, so Helen knew their relationship would go no further than mistress and lover.

One day a man named Trey Ferguson walked into the casino in Kansas City and saw her and Oswald together. He didn't like Oswald and decided to take what he had, namely, Helen O'Brien.

14.

Trey Ferguson owned one of the biggest ranches outside of Caldwell, Kansas. He ran forty-thousand head of prime beef. He hired only the roughest, toughest, meanest cowboys he could find. He also kept company of the same kind.

The rancher liked to gamble at the Cascade Casino, in Kansas City, on weekends. Kansas City was where all the action was and was where Ferguson banked his profits from the ranch, so he was often seen there on business. He was also a handsome man and woman were attracted to him.

Ferguson inherited the Leaning F Ranch from his widowed father who had spoiled him to no end. He'd gotten away with murder more than once because his father had political influence in Caldwell.

One night, at the Cascade Casino, he saw a woman on the arm of lawyer Gerald Oswald, who he had a dislike for. To him Oswald was a namby-pamby, pasty-faced wimp who wouldn't survive a single night on the range. Also, Oswald had won a litigation land dispute against him.

But it was the girl who held his interest more than Oswald did. Ferguson was struck by her beauty and poise. He knew many women before but took none of them seriously. This one was, by far, above the others. A minute after seeing her he decided to spend a few more days in the city and especially more time at the casino.

Once or twice, while on Oswald's arm, she glanced in his direction at the roulette table. Once she even smiled. He nodded in acknowledgement.

Once night he found her alone when Oswald went to buy some poker chips and cigars.

He walked up to her smiling confidently and said, "I think you're ready for a change."

She looked at him through half closed eyes and replied, "Oh? Why do you say that, good sir?"

"Because he's married and will not leave his wife. He's a dead end for you. You'll go nowhere with Oswald. I know him."

"We shall see," she said and walked away to find Oswald.

"I want you!" he said loudly as she left. She laughed.

The next night he saw them at the casino again. They were at the baccarat table and Oswald was losing heavily. Ferguson walked over and stood a few feet away, staring at Helen. Their eyes met.

She walked over to Ferguson and kissed him there and then.

Everyone looked, including her lover Oswald. He rushed over to the rancher and pulled Helen from his embrace and shook a puny little fist in his face and then challenged him to a duel.

"Don't be stupid, Oswald," Ferguson chuckled. "I was raised on a ranch. I could put a bullet between your eyes before you even knew it."

This kind of talk frightened the lawyer so he took another tact.

"Alright, Ferguson," Oswald said, "you're a gambler, I'm a gambler and we're in a place of gambling, so why not draw cards. Low card wins her."

At that moment, Helen O'Brien hated both men. If the rancher won, she would become nothing but his trophy. In fact, that's what a mistress was, wasn't it? A trophy? You hang the trophy on your wall or on your arm. It was all the same. A mistress was just a trophy to display in public, while the wife sat at home and tolerated it because she must.

Suddenly Helen felt dirty. She thought of Oswald's wife at home and hoped she was cheating on Oswald.

Ferguson got a deck of cards and he and the lawyer drew. Oswald got the lowest card and was ecstatic. He had beaten the rancher again.

"You never learn, do you, Ferguson," Oswald cried. He turned to Helen. "Shall we go, my dear?"

Helen looked at Ferguson. He shrugged and said, "The luck of the draw I'm afraid, my dear." He walked away.

The very next day Oswald was found dead in an alleyway a few blocks from his home. People thought his wife might have had him killed for cheating, but nothing came of that theory.

That was the day Ferguson called on Helen O'Brien in her apartment in the Cascade Casino.

"What do you want?" Helen asked coldly.

"Let's get married?"

"Is that how you propose to a girl?"

"Look, I have to go back to my ranch. You want to marry me or not."

"You're a son of a bitch, you know?"

"Yes or no? I'm leaving."

"Alright. Sure, why not?" Helen said. She was tired of her life. She needed a change. If it didn't work out there was always divorce.

"I don't have a warm coat," she said. "I'll need one."

A day later Helen O'Brien, wearing a new fur coat and rode in a V.I.P. car all the way to Wichita with her future husband. They stopped at Caldwell and got married by a judge who knew Trey's family and then went by buckboard to the Leaning F Ranch.

It didn't take long for Helen to discover that her marriage was not made in heaven. It was not at all like those romantic stories she read about in the romance magazines back in Chicago, where the poor girl married a prince and they live happily ever after. This marriage slowly became the marriage made in hell. Being a rancher's wife was not what she thought it would be.

For one thing, there was no honeymoon.

And second, Trey Ferguson was not what he seemed to be. His beautiful head of wavy brown hair was not real. It was a toupee. Ferguson was as bald as a rock. Each night he would remove it and place it carefully on the dresser. There were little red sores on his scalp, which he itched at during the night. He had changed from a suave, handsome devil to a hairless wonder.

There were also other surprises in store for her. He snored constantly when asleep and picked his nose when at the table eating. He spit without warning when they were walking around the ranch.

At times he became stern with her and she would lie, just to avoid an argument. It soon became a survival tool and she used it to manipulate him when she could. Once he slapped her. She put that in her little mental black book with all the other things he did to her.

He spent a lot of time in Caldwell and Kansas City. She was glad for the days he was away but also felt a need for companionship. The ranch operated around her, as if she wasn't even there.

There was one person who took an interest in her. That was Bob Hanely, the Leaning F ramrod. It was Hanely that

Helen found comfort in. He taught her how to ride and shoot whenever Ferguson was away, which was often. Did he think she was just going to sit and knit him a sweater while he was out having a good time gambling? Not Helen O'Brien-Ferguson.

Having been raised in a poor family, Helen vowed never to be poor again. To that end, she wrote herself checks using the ranch check register. She cashed them in Caldwell and had the monies sent to her account in Kansas City. It was the same account she used to hold the money her former lover Oswald gave her. She gambled that Trey would never find out. What she didn't know was that this was a high exposure crime and the criminals usually get caught.

And she soon did.

Trey Ferguson's accountant discovered the irregularities in the debit column and pointed the finger at Helen. That in itself was bad enough but when Trey caught her in a compromising position with Bob Hanely, in the barn, that was the last straw, the one that broke the camel's back

Stealing the rancher's money was one thing but making him a cuckold was another. He couldn't let that stand. The first thing that happened was the ramrod was found hanging naked and castrated a few miles outside the Leaning F Ranch on a cold day in winter.

It was Helen's turn next.

Trey devised a nasty death for her and told her how he would go about letting a few of his meaner cowboys have their fun with her before he dropped her off naked, in the mist of winter, miles from civilization, in wolf country. Just to show how much he cared for her, he would give her a boot knife to protect herself. After all, he was a gentleman.

As he had important business to attend to in Kansas City, he locked Helen in her room and told the servants to feed her only once a day and keep an eye on her until he returned. On the second day after he left, they discovered she had climbed out of the second story window, dropped down into the snow and had hitched up one of the special coaches and rode off.

She bribed two ranch hands to take to her to Ellsworth and promised them a thousand dollars each for her safe arrival.

When Trey Ferguson returned home he had the servants whipped.

15.

Some cowboys came to Junction City to die under Slade Colter's gun. At other times he went to small towns and stayed at a hotel. Usually within a day he would get a challenge. Often it was a local man or boy who felt brave and wanted attention.

Just one lucky shot and they would be known as the one who toppled the great Slade Colter. After all, he was only human and like all humans, he would have bad days, too. If someone was lucky, he could get off a quick shot and become a celebrity, a town hero.

But that bad day for Slade Colter had not yet and might never, come. And Mark Turley would keep writing his glowing tales of the great gunfighter until that day came.

After each killing, a town Marshal would come to their hotel room and respectfully request they leave and they would go somewhere else and do the same thing.

Although they traveled a lot, they always returned to Junction City to their private hotel rooms.

When Colter got a message from his old pal Verge Taggert he read it with interest and handed it to Mark Turley.

"What do you think, Turley?"

"It would be a different experience, Mr. Colter," Turley answered. "And it might make a good story."

"Yeah. Different. I'm getting bored here. Maybe a trip is in order. Do something like in the old days when I was a bounty hunter."

The offer of money was attractive. The newspapers didn't pay all that much. Colter was getting famous but not wealthy. He could use a big infusion of cash.

"Let's give it a try," Turley said. "I'll write up a day by day travelogue. That will prolong the suspense. Readers will hang on right up until the day of the big gunfight. I'll stretch it out. We'll get more money that way."

Colter chuckled. "Sounds good. I'll wire Taggert were on our way."

They rode into Danville a week after they got Taggert's telegram and took a room next to Ferguson and his crew at the hotel there. They met in Ferguson's room.

"What took you so long?" Ferguson asked.

"The snow held us up," Mark Turley said. "It was bad."

"Who are you, sir?" Ferguson asked Turley.

"He's my writer," Colter said.

"Your writer?" Trey Ferguson chuckled and turned to Taggert. "Is this the man you told me about Taggert or some show off?"

Taggert ignored the question and instead said, "Boss, this here is Slade Colter. He's here ta solve yer problem, aincha, Slade?"

Colter nodded. "Yep."

When Ferguson looked at the over six-foot-tall gunman, he knew he was looking into the eyes of a killer, a man who sold his killing skills for money. Colter saw a man who was just as cruel as he was but had a lot of money and never worked for it. This made him both envious and angry. To make it worse, he saw the rancher as a man who hired men like him to do their dirty work.

"Taggert," Ferguson said," why don't you explain to Mr. Colter what I expect him to do."

Colter's dead eyes flared up a bit.

"Why don't you tell me Ferguson or is Taggert in charge here and yer just a nobody yappin' his big mouth off?"

The remark stung Ferguson into blurting out, "No, Mr. Taggert is not in charge here, I am, sir!"

Colter chuckled. "Okay then, let's hear it."

That was too much for the rancher. He stood up.

"Mr. Taggert, I'm going down to see Bowles in the bar. Please fill Mr. Colter in on the details."

With that, the rancher stomped out of the room. Colter chuckled and walked over and plunked down on the bed, stretching out.

"An' that's yer boss?"

"Yeah."

"Stuck-up shit, ain't he?"

"Yeah. More money than brains."

"So, how much did you tell him I'd do the job fer?"

"Three grand. If it's okay, I'll take a grand."

Colter chuckled. "Five hundred is more like it."

Taggert nodded. "Okay. Five hundred."

"Does he have the cash?"

"It'll be waitin' when we git back to Ellsworth."

"What's the job?"

"Real simple. All you gotta do is brace the cowboy his wife ran off with."

"Where is he, here in town?"

"No, but we got a lead on them. They're on the ol' Oakley ta Cheyenne Wells coach road. I figure they had to hole up in Oakley because of the deep snow."

Colter nodded. "Jest make sure that pecker-head boss of yers stays out of my face."

"Sure," Taggert said.

"Who's that Bowles he went down to see?"

"He's the coachman. Ferguson doesn't go anyplace unless Bowles drives him."

Colter chuckled. "Christ! What a damn wimp!"

During all this Mark Turley sat in a corner writing how the rancher, Trey Ferguson, had hired Slade Colter to rescue his wife from an insane kidnapper.

16.

It was snowing hard when they left Danville on a gray, overcast morning. Ferguson, Taggert and Slade Colter rode inside the coach while Bowles, the driver and Mark Turley rode on top exposed to the elements.

Colter and Turley left their horses in Danville to be picked up on the way back.

Turley, a city born and bred man, wasn't use to the harsh weather of the Kansas plains. He sat shivering, holding his coat collar tight around his neck and his hat pulled down to his ears. Even with gloves on, he felt the nip and bite of the Kansas wind.

As for Bowles, his sheepskin jacket served him well, as did his leather gloves, wide brimmed hat and the pint of brandy he had stowed away in his coat pocket. From time to time he managed to take a sip. Once he handed it to Turley but Turley refused. Bowles didn't offer it any more.

By evening they rode into Sharon Springs near the Smokey Hill River and stopped. It was impossible to go on.

They had watched the road carefully for signs of travelers but saw nothing of Ferguson's wife or her companion.

There wasn't much at Sharon Springs except an old deserted stagecoach stop and a beanery surrounded by sod huts. It was mostly a hangout for cutthroats and jailbirds hiding from the law. The stage stop had been converted into a makeshift saloon that sold locally made whiskey strong enough to peel paint off of wood.

The five travelers had bean soup, biscuits and coffee at the beanery. The few people in there were all filthy scrawny looking characters who moved back into the shadows to stare at them.

After a few minutes of observing, one of them snuck out the side door and ran over to the saloon. He told of the rich visitors in the beanery stranded by the storm. His boss, recently escaped from prison, quickly set up a trap. These people would likely come in to top off their meal with a few drinks.

They waited patiently in the shadows against the far wall facing the bar. An hour later, the innocents walked in out of the storm like unsuspecting flies into a spider's web.

Taggert was the first to enter the dimly lit place. Bowles came next followed by Ferguson, Colter and Turley. They lined up at the bar and ordered drinks.

It only took Slade a few moments to read the uncertain look on the bartender's face. He turned and yelled out.

"Ambush!"

"Bowles, Taggert and Slade turned as one and drew from a crouch. Bullets crashed into the wall behind them. Exposed whisky bottles and jugs exploded, sending shards of jagged glass flying. The wall behind the bar was gouged open as slug after slug smashed into it, showering splinters all over the bar.

The defenders returned shot for shot, fanning off bullets as fast as they could. The muzzle flashes exposed the attackers lined up against the far wall like sitting ducks. Colter methodically poured shots into them. Each shot slapped an outlaw against the wall like a rag doll. Their bodies danced crazily as if on a drunken puppet master's string.

"Enough!" Colter yelled. "It's over!"

They stood up, reloaded their guns, and looked around. The air was filled with swirling gun smoke and the smell of gunpowder. Taggert looked behind the bar.

"The bartender got it," he chuckled.

Suddenly they heard a moan. An outlaw rose up from behind a table with his arms raised.

"I give up, boss," he whined.

Colter shot him between the eyes. The man fell face forward over the table and rolled onto the floor. Colter put a new bullet into his Colt.

"Anyone hurt?" the gunslinger asked.

"Mr. Bowles got it," Turley said, holding his own arm where he had taken a slight hit. Bowles lay dead on the floor.

"Where's Ferguson?" Colter asked.

"I'm here!" Ferguson said as he crawled out from under a table and dusted his clothes off. "Damn! My ears are ringing from all that noise!"

Taggert went to examine Bowles. His body was riddled with bullets and his gun was empty.

"Well," Taggert said, "at least he took a few of them jaspers with him."

The owner of the beanery came in out of the storm. He looked around and gasped.

"Shit! Look at this mess! Somebody's gotta pay!"

Colter looked at Ferguson.

"Give him some money," the gunslinger said.

"Why me? I didn't shoot the place up."

"No, you crawled into a hole like a trapped rat, you son of a bitch! Now pay the man before I shoot you in the ass!"

Ferguson and the man settled on a price and they all walked back to the beanery.

They decided to spend the night there playing cards. Taggert moved the coach around to the lee side of the building. He laid blankets over the horses and hobbled their feet.

That night, after he had his arm wrapped to stop the bleeding from his wound, Mark Turley filled five pages in his journal with flowing words that described how Slade Colter saved the cattle baron Trey Ferguson from an ambush. All by himself, Colter had dealt justice to ten attackers.

17.

When Jacob Clark killed a man in a knife fight over a woman at the age of twenty, he pleaded self-defense and went to prison for ten years. It was while he was there that he first read pamphlets put out by The Church of the Repentant Sinners.

The young man wrote them a letter saying he was a sinner and wanted to repent and get right with God. They sent him more pamphlets and even a letter from time to time.

After serving seven of the ten years in a prison outside of Chicago, Jacob was released for good behavior and on the promise he would become a good Christian. He looked for a job but no one would hire a convicted murderer when there were thousands of honest citizens looking for work.

After a year of scraping bottom Jacob Clark saw The Church of the Repentant Sinner as his only hope for survival. He found one in the Chicago suburbs and joined, not as a member but as a disciple of God.

To get into the church in this way was no simple matter. He had to take a vow of celibacy and study the Bible for five years in a monastery outside of Chicago, within view of the stockyards where they slaughtered cattle by the thousands each day. He could hear their cries of terror as he knelt and prayed to God for forgiveness for his many sins.

At the monastery, they instilled in him what a contemptible person he was, undeserving of God's forgiveness and grace. He spent many hours on his knees before the statue of Christ on the cross, lashing his back with a cat-o'-nine tail until he passed out from the pain. Many times he wished he was back in prison but when they told him he was getting closer to God's grace, he hung on.

When he finally reached the end of his tenure as a novice, he graduated to the level of assistant pastor and was given a purple robe with gold designs on it. He was assigned to assist a Pastor in a small church in the suburbs of Chicago's south side. It was close to the church's main headquarters, where they could keep an eye on him.

The Pastor's name was Cronsnoble and he was a hell-fire-and-damnation preacher. He scared the bejesus out of his flock.

Jacob's job was to set things up on the dais and lectern and sweep the church clean at the close of day and to take up the collection during Sunday's sermon.

Pastor Cronsnoble had a drinking problem. It was hard to tell if he was intoxicated or not although Jacob did detect a slight slur in his words now and then. The Pastor kept his bottle in his cubicle, next to Jacob's cubicle. Some nights the Pastor cried when he was drunk. He seemed to be a troubled man.

The people who came regularly to the Sunday sermons were all hard working people who lived in the cold-water flats in the lower class section of Chicago. Some worked in the stockyards and the smell of blood was always on them.

Others were factory workers and men who worked in the nearby coalfields west of the stockyards. The smell of coal dust and the grit of coal were forever on them, too. They sat in the small church with hopeless looks on their faces. Their lives were a dead end. There was no chance for a better life at all and they knew it and lived with it.

Jacob began to think maybe that was why the Pastor drank. Maybe he could feel their pain. They were poor yet they gave their hard-earned money to him so that God would bless them with his grace.

One day the Pastor didn't come out and Jacob found him dead in his cubicle. There was no sign of injury or foul play. It appeared as if he had willed his heart to stop beating. He was tired of it all and wanted some peace. That's all Jacob could think of.

When Jacob was promoted to the rank of Pastor, he started to think of resigning from the church. But when he saw those weary faces smiling up at him as he delivered his hellfire and damnation sermon his heart went out to them. They believed every word he said. Oh, there were a few skeptics in the crowd, but they knew they were trapped too, just like the rest.

About a year after he was promoted to Pastor, Jacob heard about the discovery of gold in eastern Colorado, just east of Cheyenne Wells. A day later he had an epiphany. Not quite a vision but an idea. He visualized a way out of this horrible life for him and those tortured souls.

After thinking about it and rolling it over in his mind and looking at it from every angle, he decided to act. That Sunday, he took the dais without opening his Bible. For a while he only stared down into their faces. They waited, wondering what was wrong. Finally, he spoke.

"My friends, the time for speaking of hope is over. The Book tells us that God helps those who help themselves. It is now time to do just that."

He could see the strange look on their faces.

"I'm going on a new adventure. If you would like, you are welcome to come with me. With God's grace we can build a new life. A life of plenty."

Jacob told them about his plan. Over the years he had saved the small salary the church gave him and now he had a goodly amount. If they would save as much as they could for a month and buy a small covered wagon, he would provide the food and equipment for panning for gold. He told them to take a week to think about it.

A week later they came back with a unanimous decision to go with him.

They left Chicago in the springtime. By autumn they were panning for gold on the slopes of a mountain ridge close to Sharon Springs, Kansas. They banked their gold in

Oakley and let it accumulate interest. The bank was most grateful for their business.

They lived on the mountain and prospered. They built a church and Jacob delivered a different kind of sermon. A sermon based on the teachings and life of Christ. Children were born in the commune, people died there and many were married there.

Life was just as Jacob had promised. Their old life soon became a fading memory. There were, of course, trials and tribulations, but that was to be expected. After all, this was still an earthly life, not a heavenly one. Over all, times were good.

That is until the evil people came with the man dressed in black wearing a red bandana.

18

Ferguson, Taggert, Colter and Turley spent the night at the beanery playing cards. In the morning, after breakfast, Taggert took up a collection. He gave the money to the owner to bury Bowles in a graveyard behind the saloon. Then they rode on.

At Oakley they stopped to look around and ask questions. Ferguson cornered an old mercantile owner.

"Have you seen a man and woman anywhere around? Or perhaps passing through?"

"No, but there's a man up on the hill where they're pannin' fer gold who said somethin' fishy."

"Like what?"

"Like a young cowboy and a beautiful woman with a fur coat. But maybe he was jest talkin'."

Ferguson smiled and chuckled.

"Yeah, sure. He was probably just talking. Where can I find this man?"

The man scratched his chin and thought.

"Well, you go west about six miles and you'll see a road off to the left. That's where they live. Up there on the south slope. About a mile up They been pannin' fer gold up there fer years. They live there."

"Thank you sir," Ferguson said.

Later he met the others over by the stable. They could tell by the look on his face he had learned something.

"I've got the bitch at last!" Ferguson cried. "She's up in the hills with a bunch of gold prospectors."

"Where exactly?" Taggert asked.

"Six miles down the line."

Mark Turley shivered and looked up. Snow clouds were roiling in a low, lead colored sky. The wind picked up.

They started off again and made their way slowly along the road through the densely falling snow. Taggert drove the coach. Ferguson, Colter and Turley rode inside. At times he went off the road into a ditch, almost overturning the small vehicle. Those inside bounced around.

"For Christ sakes, Taggert!" Ferguson yelled. "Watch what you're doing, man!"

"Screw you, you ass hole," Taggert said to himself.

Inside the coach Ferguson and Colter sat ignoring each other. Finally, Turley spoke.

"You got the money, Mr. Ferguson?"

"You sound like a pimp, Mr. Turley. Is that what you are, Mr. Colter's pimp?"

"Watch yer mouth, Ferguson," Colter growled.

Ferguson chuckled.

"Don't worry, I have your blood money, sir," he sneered. He placed his hand over the left breast of his coat and patted it. "It's right here."

"So it's my blood money, is it?" Colter growled. "And yer hands are clean, are they?" The gunslinger laughed. "You self-righteous bastard! Fer two bits I'd plug yer ass right along with the cowboy's."

"And my wife," Ferguson said boldly. "I'm paying you for taking care of her, too."

"Of course," Colter chuckled." And what a brave man you are."

"After this is finished, I don't ever want to see you again, sir!"

"Maybe ya will and maybe ya won't. We'll see about that later." Colter chuckled.

These words sent a chill through Ferguson. He fingered the derringer he had in his coat pocket.

It took them two hours to cover the six miles to the side road leading up the slope of the mountain. Taggert struggled to get the horses turned but they finally were in a position to ascend the steep narrow incline. He snapped the reins and the horses strained against the wind. Several times the trail made a switchback to avoid landslides. The animals often lost their footing on the snow covers rocks.

At last, they came to a level open area where the panning camp was. Taggert got down and opened the coach door. They all stood there in the falling snow looking around at the buildings. Not a soul was in sight.

"Anybody here?" Taggert yelled out.

Old Jacob came out of the long building with the cross over the door and waved.

"Hello, strangers," the old man said, smiling. "Would ya like ta come in an' join us fer supper?"

"Why, thank you sir," Ferguson said, returning the smile. "That is very civil of you."

They followed the old man into the shelter of the building. It was warm inside and lit by oil lamps hanging from the rafters. They could smell the aroma of mutton-turnip stew, fresh baked bread and wild strawberry tarts. The fumes from hot coffee came off the big table.

Those already eating stopped to stare at the newcomers, especially at Slade Colter in his fancy black outfit. Some turned and whispered to each other. They knew what he was. A hired killer.

"Please sit," old Jacob said. "Our food ain't fancy but it's hot, an' you all look like you kin use a good thawin' out."

People shifted over to make room for them. Turley and Taggert sat between two men. Ferguson sat next to Jacob and Colter sat between two young boys who couldn't take their eyes off his guns.

Hot bowls of steaming stew were carried in from the kitchen and set before the guests. They ate as if starved, soaking the last drop of stew up with bread. The meal closed with a cup of coffee and a wild strawberry tart. After that they talked.

"If ya don't mind my askin', what brings you all up here on the mountain this time of year?" Jacob asked. "Jest curious is all."

"My wife," Ferguson said quickly. "She's been taken by force and we're looking for her."

The room went very quiet. A cold silence set in for a moment then murmurs echoed around the table.

"Whatta ya gonna do when ya find 'em?" Someone asked.

"Take her home," Ferguson said, smiling. "Just take her home. Her children miss her very much."

"And the man who took her? Whatta ya gonna do ta him?"

"Well take him to Oakley and turn him over to the Marshal there," Ferguson answered innocently.

A man further down the table spoke up.

"Why haven't you brought the Marshal with you? Seems like Marshal Rogers should be takin' action on this."

Ferguson was caught off balance and he said the first thing that crossed his mind.

"He couldn't come. His wife is sick. So he sent a deputy."

Ferguson pointed at Slade Colter.

"Thet's a good one! The Marshal's wife died last year. He's a widower," someone said and chuckled. "You must be seein' ghosts, mister!"

"Marshal Rogers doesn't have a deputy," another one said. "The town can't afford one!"

"I don't see no badge," a woman said. "Tell him ta show us a badge."

Suddenly Slade Colter shouted, "Enough of this crap!" He grabbed the boy on his left, drew his gun and pointed it at his head. "I'll count to three and somebody better start talkin'." A woman moaned and fainted.

Ten minutes later a man was leading Ferguson, Taggert, Colter and Turley up the hill through the falling snow.

19.

The young cowboy and Helen Ferguson were sitting before the hearth fire holding hands when the door flew open and Ferguson burst in.

"Helen, my love!"

"Trey?"

She jumped up quickly with a terrified look on her face. The cowboy got up slower and stood staring as Taggert, Colter and Mark Turley came in and shut the door. The kid glanced over at his gun belt hanging from a peg on the wall by the hearth.

"Don't try it kid," Taggert said. His gun was already out.

Colter stared at the young cowboy and chuckled.

"Christ, is this what all the fuss is about? A damn kid?"

"Hello, Helen," Ferguson said sweetly. "It's so good to see you again, my darling. I missed you so very much." He broke out laughing sarcastically.

"Leave me alone, Trey!" Helen cried, almost pleading. "Please leave me alone!"

"Now, is that any way to talk to your husband? By the way, why don't you introduce me to your young friend here?"

"His name is Edward Barnes," she said, her voice breaking. "He saved me when my coach tipped over."

"I see. And he took you miles away from home," Ferguson said. "I think that's called kidnapping" He turned to Taggert. "What do you say, Taggert? Isn't that called kidnapping?"

"It is in my book," Taggert chuckled.

Ferguson stared at Barnes. "Are you a kidnapper, young man?"

"No, sir," Barnes said seriously. "It's agin the code."

"Well, of course it is," Ferguson said loudly in a very condescending voice. "You're not so stupid after all." Then, after a withering, patronizing stare, "Do you know what they do to kidnappers when they are caught?"

"They hang 'em sir," the young man said. There was a slight tremble in his voice. Helen gave him a sorrowful glance.

"Indeed they do!" the rancher said in a lawyerly way.

Taggert chuckled. He was enjoying this.

"He didn't kidnap me, Trey," Helen said. "After you sent those two men to kill me on the road, I asked him for help."

"Oh, then he's just an innocent fool, is he?"

"Stop it, Trey!" she yelled. "Just go away!"

Ferguson walked slowly over to his wife.

"How about a nice kiss, darling?"

The rancher grabbed his wife by the hair, twisted her head sideways and mashed his mouth against hers in a grinding, brutal kiss. He held it for a moment then gasped and shoved her back against the wall by the hearth. His lip was dripping blood where she bit him.

"You bitch!"

Ferguson struck out with his open palm and slapped Helen hard on the side of her face. She moaned and sank to her knees.

The cowboy shook his head and lashed out with a fist that caught the rancher square on the jaw. His hat flew off and he staggered backwards holding his face, crying out in pain. Ferguson reached into his coat for his derringer. He had it out when Colter drew his gun and pointed it at Ferguson's head.

"Drop it ass hole!"

Ferguson was confused. "What?"

"Drop it or I'll blow a hole in that stupid head of yours!"

Colter walked over to the rancher, grabbed the derringer from his hand and tossed it into a far corner.

Ferguson rubbed his jaw. He glared defiantly at Colter and strutted over to Helen, facing her.

"I have a mistress in Kansas City. After I get rid of you, I'll have her take your place at the ranch!" He spat the words at her. "You're dead!"

"Go to hell, Trey," the woman said. Her right hand flew up across his face and grabbed a handful of his hair and yanked the toupee off his head and tossed it into the fire. It burst into flames giving off a horrible stench.

The rancher growled, clenched his fist and made to strike Helen again but stopped when the cowboy jumped in front of her.

Colter burst out laughing. He laughed long and hard. He pointed a finger at Ferguson's baldhead.

"Damn, man, you sure shed fast!" he yelled. Taggert stifled a chuckle and turned his head away.

The rancher's face turned purple with rage. He pointed a finger at Helen and the cowboy.

"Kill them! That's what I'm paying you for!" He screamed at Colter. "Just don't stand there looking stupid!"

"The kid, yeah, but not the woman," the gunslinger replied. "She's yer problem."

"I'll not pay you then!"

"You will if you wanna leave this hill alive, my friend," Colter said calmly. "Now you stand right there until I tell you to move."

For a moment, the rancher glared at the gunslinger then grabbed his hat from the floor and stood staring hatefully at his wife.

Colter, with his gun still out, walked over to the cowboy, reached down, and got his boot knife. He looked around until he found the boy's lariat and cut two pieces from it. He handed them to Taggert.

"Tie the woman and the kid up," Colter said. He stared at the rancher. "And if you don't behave I'll tie you up, too, understand? You're starting to get on my nerves." Colter stepped away.

The rancher nodded and sat in a chair and sulked.

Taggert tied Helen and the cowboy up, leaving them lying on the floor in front of the hearth. He then went and sat in a chair at the table. Colter sat on one bunk and Mark Turley on the other. Ferguson sat quietly brooding in the other chair nearby.

"Let's get some sleep," Colter said. "Tomorrow we'll finish this up good and proper and go home."

Mark Turley sat on the bunk writing in his journal. He was excited. Tomorrow Slade Colter would brace the cowboy and make his thirty-fifth kill.

20

The cowboy and Helen managed to doze off from time to time. Even though the fire in the hearth went out, they stayed close enough to combine their body heat. Helen's fur coat helped a lot to fight off the cold. The wind howled around the cabin walls and snow crept in through the cracks.

Taggert rebuilt the fire after dawn and untied Helen and the cowboy. She cut up some bacon and fried it, then used the grease to cook some flour biscuits. There weren't enough tin plates and cups to go around so they took turns using the two they had. It went slow but finally everyone had eaten.

"Well, kid," Colter said to the cowboy, "you ready?"

"Sure. Jest hand me my gun and we'll have it out," Ed Barnes said eagerly. "Let's do it!"

Colter chuckled. "Sure, but let's you and me talk first."

The gunslinger had the young man sit at the table with him. Mark Turley sat on a bunk nearby with his journal open and his pencil in hand.

"Where you from, kid?' Slade asked. His piercing eyes drilled into the cowboy's.

Turley started to write.

"Texas," Edward Barnes said.

"Where in Texas?"

"Clifton."

"Clifton? Never heard of it. What's it near?"

"Waco. On the Brazos River."

Ferguson scowled. "Are you going to shoot him or talk him to death, Colter?"

Colter grimaced at the rancher. "First things first. This has to be done right. I've got a reputation to consider." He turned back to the cowboy and adjusted his bright red bandana. The young man stared at it, fascinated. He had never seen one with little white stars on it before.

"So, yer from around Waco, huh?"

"Yes, sir."

"Then I'll call you the Waco Kid. Would you like that?"

Barnes shrugged. "I don't care what ya call me, mister."

"Colter. My name is Slade Colter. Maybe you've heard about me?"

The young man shrugged. "No sir, can't say as I have."

Colter chuckled. "That's okay. After today it won't matter one way or the other, as far as you're concerned."

"Come on, Colter!" Ferguson yelled. "Just kill him so we can get the hell out of this damn place!"

"All in due time, Mr. Ferguson," Colter said. He went back to questioning the cowboy.

"How many men have you killed, Waco?"

Edward Barnes thought that over. "I shot one man in the back who was tryin' ta kill Mrs. Ferguson. An' three others. Thet's about all I kin admit to, Mr. Colter."

The gunman stroked his chin. "Hmmmm. We'll have to fix that." He looked over at Mark Turley. "Make that fifteen, Mr. Turley. Put down that the Waco Kid killed his first man when he was fourteen and had killed fourteen more by the time he was sixteen.

"Sure," Turley said as he wrote in his journal. "Whatever you say, Mr. Colter."

Taggert chuckled. He was enjoying the whole thing. This simple-minded kid didn't even know he was helping write his own obituary.

"This is bullshit!" Ferguson yelled. "Pure bullshit! Just kill the simpleminded fool!"

"Relax. I wanna to do this proper and legal. I won't have it said that Slade Colter gunned down a no-nothing piss ant from nowhere. It would ruin my reputation," Colter said.

"To hell with your reputation, you egotistical bastard!"

Ferguson ran over to the corner and snatched up his derringer and aimed it at Barnes. Helen screamed. There was a gun blast but it wasn't the derringer. Slade Colter had drawn with lightning speed and shot Trey Ferguson in the heart. He fell backwards and sat against the wall staring with vacant eyes.

"Damn!" Taggert said. "It looks like I'm out of a job!" He walked over to Ferguson's body and felt in his coat for the money. "There's nothing here. The lying bastard!" He went over by the hearth and rolled a cigarette.

Colter put his gun away and turned his attention once again to the young cowboy.

"Did I hear you just challenge me, cowboy?"

Barnes looked confused. He looked around. "No sir, I didn't challenge nobody, Mr. Colter."

"You heard him, didn't you Taggert?"

Taggert shrugged. He wasn't very happy over Colter shooting his boss and putting him out of an easy job. It wasn't in the plan. He looked away and said nothing.

For a moment Slade Colter was wondering what was going on in Taggert's mind. He turned to Mark Turley.

"You heard it, didn't you, Mr. Turley?"

Mark Turley stopped writing. He kept looking down at his journal. Suddenly he felt very dirty. This young cowboy had meant well by helping a woman. Now he was about to be led like a lamb to the slaughter. He wasn't trying to get a reputation as a fast gun by bracing Colter. Slade Colter would kill him and Turley would write lies about it.

Colter suddenly got up, walked over to Helen Ferguson, and slapped her hard, so hard her head cracked against the wall near the hearth.

Barnes saw it and stood up. He was strangely calm.

"I'll have ta kill you fer that, Mr. Colter," he said. His words almost sounded ridiculously stupid.

"There. You heard it, Mr. Turley. The Waco Kid just challenged me! Write it down."

Mark Turley wrote nothing. He sat frozen on the cot staring down at the journal as if it seeing it for the first time. He heard Colter taunting the boy. Turley had never seen this side of his mentor before.

"Where do you want me to put it, kid?" Colter said confidently. "In the left eye or the right one? Between the eyes? In the mouth? You ever see a man shot in the mouth, kid?" The kid didn't answer. "No? Well, you should. The bullet breaks off the front teeth as it goes in and cuts the spinal cord at the neck as it goes out. It isn't pretty. Maybe that's where I'll put yours."

Mark Turley looked up to see the young cowboy get his gun belt off the peg. He slowly buckled it on and walked outside into the howling wind and snow. Colter followed, chuckling.

Helen Ferguson began to tremble, not with cold, but with fear. She let out a loud wailing sob and broke down crying. Mark Turley came over to her and put an arm around her. He was crying, too.

Taggert went to the door and opened it a little to look out. He wanted to see the free show.

It wasn't snowing very hard as the boy walked from the cabin. Colter stood ten feet from the door and waited. When the cowboy was about forty feet away from him, he shouted.

"There, kid! That's about good."

Edward Barnes turned and looked around.

White spirals of snow danced across the yard between him and Slade Colter. Crows sat in the nearby birch trees, stark black against the white bark. They seemed to be watching. They turned their heads to chatter to one another.

"Is that distance okay for you, kid?" Colter asked.

The young man only nodded. He stood relaxed, as if knowing it was all over for him anyway. No use fighting it.

Colter called back to the cabin. "This is gonna make a great story, Mr. Turley. You can call it, Slade Colter and the Waco Kid." He looked back at Edward Barnes. "You'll be famous too, after this, cowboy."

The wind whipped the cowboy's long hair. His shirt snapped like a sheet in the wind.

"No hard feelings kid." Colter was milking it to the end, enjoying every minute of it. The wind was blowing harder now and he had to shout to overcome it. "I'll let you start your draw. That's fair, right?" When he got no reaction from the boy, he decided to end it and shouted.

"Draw!"

An angry gust of wind picked up a thick pile of snow and sent it rolling across the yard. It almost blinded Edward Barnes. All he could see was that bright red bandana. It stood out like a blazing beacon in a stormy sea, beckoning to him, a signpost in a wall of white.

As he sighted his gun on that red triangle, something jolted his left upper thigh and he heard the roar of Colter's Colt against the wind. A numbness crept along his leg followed by the searing heat of a red-hot poker. The cowboy started to fall sideways but managed to fan off three quick shots before he hit the ground.

The red spot seemed to move from side to side then float slowly downward onto the snow-covered ground. A sea of crows screamed at the wind and flew upward like a black cloud. They circled once and reclaimed their places in the trees.

Inside the cabin, Taggert heard three sickening thuds against flesh. He looked out to see Colter drop to the ground.

"Son of a bitch!" he yelled and threw the door open and started to draw his gun.

"Don't do that!"

Helen Ferguson pointed a derringer at him. He waited undecided for a moment then finished pulling his gun.

They both fired at the same time. His bullet hit her in the chest and hers hit him in his gun arm. He dropped his Colt. Helen held her chest and sat down on the floor looking pale. The light slowly faded from her eyes.

Taggert yelled at Mark Turley. "Turley! Get my gun!"

Mark Turley started to cry. He stood in front of Taggert and looked at him as if seeing him for the first time.

"Damn it, Turley! Hand me my gun, man!"

Turley wipe tears from his eyes and slowly bent down to pick up Taggert's gun. He held it in his hand staring at it. Shaking his head and sobbing, he shot Taggert in the heart.

After that he dropped the Colt and walked over to cradle Helen Ferguson in his arms.

Edward Barnes came limping into the cabin. He saw Helen and groaned. He struggled over and grabbed her up in his arms and kissed her forehead again and again, moaning and wailing.

"Taggert was going to blindside you. She stopped him cold," Turley sobbed. "She was magnificent."

Turley stood up and walked over to the cot. He picked up his journal, took it over to the hearth and dropped it into the dying fire. For a few moments he stood watching as it crackled and burst into flames.

He got a blanket and put it over Mrs. Ferguson and the cowboy to keep them warm.

21

They heard voices out in the yard. Mark Turley went to see who it was. He saw old Jacob and two men standing by Slade Colter's body, staring down at it. Turley motioned for them to come into the cabin.

"We heard shooting," the old man said.

When they saw Helen in the arms of the cowboy, they took their hats off.

"Is she daid?" one of the men asked.

Mark Turley nodded.

Jacob noticed the bodies of Taggert and Ferguson.

"A lot went on here, didn't it?"

"More than you can imagine sir," Turley said, wiping his eyes.

The old man walked slowly over to where Barnes was holding Helen tight in his arms, rocking her gently.

"She's in God's hands now, son," Jacob said gently. The cowboy looked up at him. "We'll give her a proper burial."

"Thank you, sir."

"An' I'll say a special sermon, too."

Barnes nodded. "I'd be grateful."

The old preacher stared at Taggert and Ferguson.

"Were these men evil?"

"Yes," the cowboy muttered.

"I thought as much. I knew they was evil when I first laid eyes on them. We'll bury 'em up here and forget 'em."

Mark Turley walked out into the yard and stared down at Colter. It wasn't snowing now and the wind had swept the snow from the gunslinger's face. His eyes were open. The raging fire to kill was now replaced by the dull blank stare of the dead.

"Your time finally came, didn't it?" Turley yelled.

He began to laugh hysterically. The wind carried his voice across the yard into the birch trees. The crows heard it and cawed mockingly. They had witnessed man's inhumanity to man. Now they mocked him.

The journalist bent down slowly and untied the red bandana. The wind snapped at it, trying to pull it from his hands. He stared down at Colter.

"You took it from a dead man and now I'm taking it from you," Turley said. "Goodbye Mr. Colter."

Turley stuffed the bandana quickly into his jacket pocket, leaving some of it hanging out. He scampered back into the cabin clapping his hands to warm them.

Jacob's two men took a cot from the corner and set it in the middle of the room. They wrapped Helen's body securely in a blanket, laid her on the cot and then took it outside into the yard. On the way back into the cabin they picked up Colter's body and put it on the floor alongside Taggert and Ferguson.

"Everybody out," Jacob said.

Everyone went out into the yard except him. They heard him praying and a few moments later they smelled smoke. The old man came rushing out just as the cabin began to go up in flames.

"May ye burn in Hades for ever and ever!" He yelled, shaking his fist at the building.

The two men picked up the cot and followed Jacob down the hill. The old preacher and Mark Turley helped the cowboy along.

As they went down the slope, they felt the warmth at their backs and heard the crackling flames roaring behind them. The dry wood of the cabin exploded in the intense heat. Crows in the birches cawed and flew away, frightened by the fire.

22.

Bessy Watts was working in the commune kitchen when four mysterious intruders arrived that cold snowy evening. She was very busy but she did get a chance to glance out into the eating area once or twice to see what all the fuss was about. She never got a look at the strangers but did see a flash of red once. She paid it no mind at the time and went about her business. Later she learned that these people had demanded to see the young cowboy and his wife.

Back on that first day when he came, the young cowboy caught her staring at him several times. Once he even smiled at her. There was something about him that reminded her of her brother Tommy. Maybe it was the way he walked. He was tall and lean like him and had a bashful smile just like her brother.

No one slept very well that night because of the evil intruders with their guns. Jacob took the grownups aside and they talked late into the night.

"Those men up there," Jacob said. "I think they came to harm the boy and the women. I'm almost sure of it."

"They threatened my little boy," one said.

"They're evil men," a man growled.

"Maybe they'll harm us too before they leave," a woman cried.

Another said, "We'll, maybe if we leave them alone they'll just go away."

Old Jacob nodded. "That may be the case, but what about the boy and the woman? Are we to just stand by and do nothing?"

No one said anything because no one wanted any trouble. They just wanted it to go away. They were God fearing, gentle people and wanted to live in peace.

Jacob said nothing more. They all went to bed but did not sleep well. They were afraid these men would harm them or the children before they left.

In the morning at the breakfast table they heard gunshots from the cabin up above the slope.

"They're killing the boy and the woman!" someone sobbed. "Oh, God!"

"Maybe we're next!" someone else cried.

"Will they kill us before they go, too?" another worried.

"They came for them, not us, you fool!" someone shouted.

Bessy Watts stood up at the table.

"I'm going up there," she said. She was thinking about the young cowboy. "I'm not afraid of them or their guns!"

"No," Jacob said. "It's my place to go." He got up.

"I'll go with you," a man said.

"I'll go, too," another said.

"Take the shotgun with you," someone yelled. It was the only weapon they had.

"No, no guns," Jacob said. "No guns."

In half an hour, Jacob and the two men left the commune and started up the snowy slope to the cabin. Everyone stood watching until they were out of sight. Some people left to attend to chores, but most stood in the open area staring upward waiting anxiously to see what was going to happen next, if at all. Bessy Watts was among those who waited.

An hour went by.

Finally, they saw movement at the top. Jacob and the man called Turley held the cowboy up between them as they came slowly down the slope. The boy's left leg was bloody and bandaged. The other two commune men came behind them carrying a cot with a body on it. Everyone knew it was the woman. The wind tugged at long strands of hair that fell out from beneath the blanket.

It was then that Bessy Watts saw the red bandana with the star sewn into the corner sticking out of Turley's pocket. She said nothing at the time, deciding to wait for a better moment.

The commune carpenter made a pine box for Helen Ferguson and they placed her in it with her expensive fur coat and nailed the top on. Jacob read the appropriate verses from the Bible and gave a sermon of his own about angels and chariots taking her to heaven's Elysian Fields in a far paradise. The young cowboy bent his head in sorrow.

A day after the sermon and burial, after breakfast, Bessy Watts spoke to Mr. Turley.

"Mr. Turley, sir," she said. "Is that a red bandana I see in your coat pocket?"

"Yes, it is," the journalist said.

"And does it have a white star sewn into each corner, sir?"

"Why, yes it does," Turley answered in surprise. "How did you know?"

"I know a lot about thet bandana, sir," Bessy Watts said. "It will turn out to be twenty-seven inches by twenty-seven inches square too, I think, if you measure it."

"How would you know that?" a man asked.

"Because I made thet bandana fer my brother Tommy some months ago. It was stolen from him when he was murdered."

The room quickly fell very quiet. Everyone stared from Bessy Watts to Mark Turley who, for the moment, seemed to be at a loss for words. He slowly reached into his pocket, pulled the red bandana out and opened it up. Everyone stared at it.

"Where did you git it, sir?" Bessy asked bluntly. "If I may ask?"

"Ah, well, I took it off of Mr. Colter."

"Do you know who he got it from, sir?"

"From a man he killed in Junction City."

Someone in the crowd chuckled and said, "Aw, she's jest a makin' it up so she kin git a free bandany!"

"No, she ain't," a woman replied. "Bessy told me how she made one fer her twin brother a while back an' now there it is!"

"It's a miracle!" someone shouted.

Mark Turley handed the bandana to Bessy Watts.

"There must be a great story behind it," Turley said. "I'd like to tell it to the world."

"You a word-smith, mister?" someone asked.

"Yes. I'm a journalist," Turley said. He looked at Bessy. "Can we talk about this later?"

"Sure, if ya want to."

A few days later, after interviewing Bessy Watts, Mark Turley got Bowles' saddle from the boot of the Ferguson coach, saddled up one of the coach horses and rode out on a quest to write the complete story of the red bandana. He stopped in Oakley to send a wire about the story. The Kansas City Star gave him a commission and he headed for the Storeyville area to see the Marshal who had handled the investigation into the murder of Tommy Watts. He didn't know where that would lead, but it was a place to start. Bessy told him to take the red bandana if he wanted and he did.

After Turley left, old Jacob took the young girl aside.

"Thet poor cowboy has a busted heart," he said. "Maybe you kin kinda stay with him a while so he don't feel so all alone. Will ya do thet, Bess?"

"Yes, Jacob, I will," the girl replied.

Bessy Watts smiled inwardly because now she had a reason to be close to the handsome young man. In the following days she made it her mission to nurse the wounded cowboy back to health. She cleaned and put fresh bandages on his leg every day and became his crutch as he tried to walk. In two weeks she had him back on his feet.

During that time, they talked a lot He told her how he had met Helen Ferguson that fateful day on the old coach road east of Danville and how he felt he had to protect her.

"Then she wasn't yer wife?"

"No ma'am. But we didn't live in sin. You believe me, don't ya, ma'am."

"Yes," Bessy said, glad to hear the words. "I kinda thought thet. Did ya love her?"

"Well, I respected her an' I wanted ta protect her. She seemed kinda lost and sorta lonely."

"She was very beautiful."

"Yes, she was."

In the passing days, Bessy learned that the cowboy couldn't read or write and began giving him lessons. They spent a lot of time together and she became attach to him.

"Are you gonna leave us?" she asked.

"Do ya want me to?"

"No."

"Then I won't go." He held her hand. "I'll stay until ya tell me to leave."

"I won't."

"Maybe ya will."

"No I won't!" she insisted.

They both laughed.

"Let's go for a walk," he said.

He took Bessy Watt's hand. They walked slowly up the slope, stopping to pick holly and mistletoe on the way. The sun was shining and the snow was beginning to melt. Crows were on the ground pecking at the exposed earth.

When the crows saw them coming, they complained and flew upward, sparkling in the sunlight like black diamonds.

The End.

About the Author

As a young boy growing up in the city, the author never passed up a chance to see a western movie. His heroes were Buck Jones, Johnny Mack Brown, Wild Bill Elliot and John Wayne, to name a few. As an adult, he often wondered where his love of westerns came from. Perhaps it has something to do with his grandfather, John L. Annan, who was a cowboy from Helena, Montana, in days of old.

R. Annan is a seasoned and traveled author with many interests. As a career serviceman, he served in Korea and Vietnam. He also completed a one-year course at the Defense Language Institute at Monterey, California and graduated from the University of South Florida with a B.A. in Art and Art History. After taking a two-year course in screenwriting at the Hollywood Scriptwriting Institute, he established *The Old Time Radio Club Time Machine* as both a scriptwriter and an actor.

A Note from the Author

Thank you for reading my book. If you enjoyed it, would you please consider rating and reviewing it? Thank you!

16888103R00075

Printed in Great Britain
by Amazon